J0B70554

A Gift For:

From:

Copyright © 2017 Hallmark Licensing, LLC

Published by Hallmark Gift Books,
a division of Hallmark Cards, Inc.,
Kansas City, MO 64141
Visit us on the Web at Hallmark.com.

All rights reserved. No part of this publication may be reproduced,
transmitted, or stored in any form or by any means without the prior
written permission of the publisher.

Editorial Director: Delia Berrigan
Art Director: Chris Opheim
Designer: Ren-Whei Harn
Production Designer: Dan Horton
Contributing Writers: Ren-Whei Harn, Kait Jerome,
Megan Reed, and Valerie Stark

ISBN: 978-1-63059-740-5
BOK1097

Made in China
0219

ADULTING
So
Hard

By
Kara Goodier

Hallmark

So THIS is Being an Adult: An Introduction

When I was a kid, I always thought people just woke up one day feeling . . . older. That you woke up filled with confidence and answers and wisdom beyond your years (or with the know-how to fold a fitted sheet, at least). But I realized that, as years went on, I still felt like the same kid. There went my notion that turning into a grown-up was an overnight process, or at least a process where you could reach "the end" and feel like a *real* grown-up. And as I talked to people around me, it seemed like I wasn't alone in this: nobody feels like an adult full-time.

We're all a little lost, flying by the seat of our pants and hoping to figure it out as we go. It's an awkward process, learning to balance responsibilities with the enjoyable parts of life. But you can still find the room for fun, and mastering that balance is part of "adulting."

But maybe there's no such thing as growing up. After all, being an "adult" looks completely different depending on who you ask—and it's not just generational differences. Some people are all about their "binge-watch and chill" life, while others strive for the perfect Instagram post about their latest travels and adventures. But let's be real: laundry is a chore AND a bore. Doing dishes and paying bills is no one's idea of a fun time. These are things we can all agree on.

So when do you consider yourself an adult? When you get your own place (with or without a roommate)? When you buy a house, get engaged, or get married? When you start a family? (Fur babies count, too.) Who knows? And, really, who's to say? Becoming an adult is not new phenomena—and even if the road looks a bit different today, there are still the same speed bumps we all have to go over. So keep talking about hating the DMV line and grocery shopping, and being confused about basic cooking skills, because it's good to know we aren't alone in this.

That being said, I wanted to put together a book full of relatable reminders and helpful hints about the adult world. Hopefully, with a bit of guidance and a lot of laughs, you'll join me in the journey of ADULTING SO HARD.

Let the adulting fun begin!
~ Kara

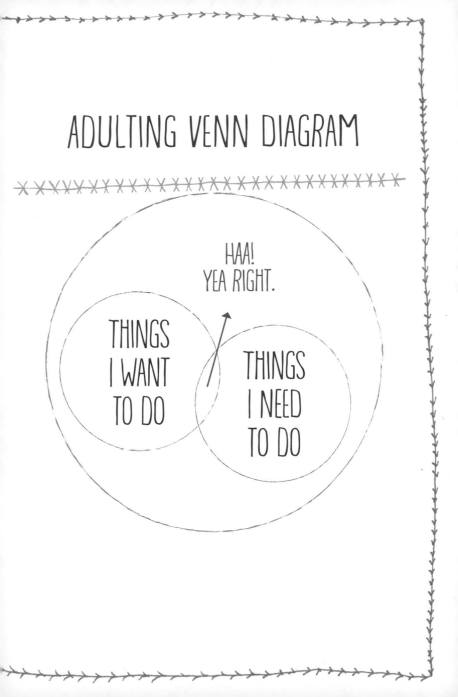

PROS AND CONS OF
PLANNING YOUR OWN MEALS

PRO	CON

You can eat anything for any meal.

You can eat ANY THING for ANY MEAL.

TACO
TIME

*

DRINK *

DONUT

yum
SCRUM

At some point, you gotta learn self restraint.

FOLDING A FITTED SHEET

i swear, this should be an Olympic sport. After asking my mom to show me at least 8 times and then watching countless YouTube videos on the topic, i STILL haven't mastered folding a fitted sheet. People who can do this effortlessly are magicians.

Folding a Fitted Sheet:
A HOW-TO

STEP 1: Stick your hands into the top two corners, wearing them like inside-out mittens (the seams should be showing on the corners).

STEP 2: Fold the sheet in half vertically, and flip the right corner over the left corner like it's a pocket. (Match the corner seams, like you're clapping, and then flip your right mitten over the left.)

STEP 3: Repeat this step on other end—put one corner inside the other, making sure the sheet remains folded in half vertically.

STEP 4: Fold the sheet in half horizontally to join all four corners—flip the right set of corners over the left set of corners. All four corners should be sitting inside each other like Pringles® at this point.

STEP 5: Fold the curved edge in towards the center a bit so it creates a straight edge, then fold the now-rectangle sheet however you prefer. (I prefer to fold in half, then fold that into thirds.)

OPTIONAL STEP: Use a pillowcase from the sheet set to store the fitted sheet, flat sheet, and other pillowcase to keep your closet tidy.

I MISS YOSHI

Nintendo®

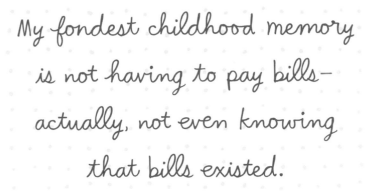

My fondest childhood memory
is not having to pay bills—
actually, not even knowing
that bills existed.

Those were the REAL glory days.

As an adult,
I can do
WHATEVER
I want...
but I always
end up just
wanting to
go home and

take a nap.

ZZZ

When I was younger,
my inner voice would say,

"YOU PROBABLY
SHOULDN'T SAY THAT."

Now it just says,

"EH, LET'S SEE
WHAT HAPPENS."

THE FACT THAT I'M
CONSIDERED AN ADULT
IS BOTH HILARIOUS
AND WORRYING.

Adulthood is like
the carnival, and we're
all just kids excited by
the rides and the candy
until we realize we can't
find our parents.

Even Netflix judges
me now for how
many episodes
of one show
I can watch in a row.

BUILDING GOOD CREDIT

This is one of those frustrating cycles where you can't get a credit card until you have good credit, but you can't build good credit without getting . . . a credit card (or other type of credit line). But building a good credit score will help you apply for loans, apartments, mortgages, and more in your later adult years. Plus, managing money responsibly is a good skill to have, regardless of your financial goals.

DO:

- Start with a student card or secured card. These are typically backed by a small savings account or certificate of deposit to establish and build good credit.

- Only charge up to 30% of your credit limit (the max) to your card—and **pay it off, on time, every month.**

- Grow your credit knowledge, and know the difference between a hard and soft inquiry on your credit report.

> Tip: It takes about 2 years to build a decent credit score, so start the work before you need it.

DON'T:

- Don't just make the minimum payments—you'll end up paying way more in interest. Pay whatever you can, whenever you can to avoid larger statement balances and lower credit usage.

- Don't buy what you can't afford or pay off quickly.

- Don't open a lot of credit accounts just to build credit. Having fewer credit accounts for longer is better than having a lot of newer credit accounts.

You can't choose your family, or change them. You can only love them for who they are and the role they play in your life, whatever that role is. With any luck, they'll do the same for you.

The other good news is that you can choose your friends. And friends count as family, too. Celebrate them (maybe host a Friendsgiving) and let them know how much they're appreciated, because they're going through this crazy journey with you.

I WORK HARD TO
MAKE SURE MY KIDS
HAVE A GOOD LIFE.

(So what that my kids
have four legs and fur.)

ALL MY FRIENDS ARE POSTING ABOUT HAVING BABIES AND GETTING PROMOTED AND I'M JUST OVER HERE EATING LEFTOVERS FOR BREAKFAST AT NOON.

Get outside into nature.

There will be days when it all piles up, because work and life always seem to unravel at the same time. When this happens, set down your phone and step outside. Get some fresh air and remind yourself just how big this world is. There are some problems that will take a lot of work and effort. But most things are not as big as they seem.

ME:

has 42 things on my to-do list,
17 emails to reply to,
is falling behind on having
friends and a social life,
and is running out of budget.

ALSO me:
*curled up in front of the tv
with a pint of ice cream*
"This is fine."

GETTING WRINKLES OUT OF CLOTHES

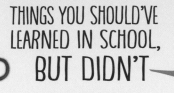

i have owned an iron for 3 years and have only ever used it once (and it was for a craft project, not clothes). The fact is, if you can get your clothes out of the dryer quick enough, they typically won't wrinkle. However, there's nothing that says, "i've given up trying" more than a nice outfit that's ruined by wrinkles. So if you have some wrinkly clothes, but don't necessarily want to break out the iron (if you even have one), here are three ways to get rid of those wrinkles.

Ironing Hacks

IN 15 MINUTES OR LESS

Option 1

Toss the wrinkled clothes in a dryer with an ice cube for about 15 minutes.

Option 2

Make a makeshift steam room. Hang the wrinkly clothes in the bathroom (close to shower, without them getting wet), turn on a hot shower, close the bathroom door, and wait 15 minutes.

Option 3

Girls, your flatiron is about to become your favorite multipurpose tool: A few quick passes on a small section of clothing can help a wrinkly collar or hem lay flat in seconds.

EXTRA STRENGTH

As kids, we wondered
why our parents
were always
in a bad mood.
Now we're like . . .

OOOOOHHHHHH.

PROS AND CONS OF
HAVING AN INCOME

PRO	CON
You can buy ANYTHING you want.	That might mean having to eat ramen for the last 28 days of the month.

I LOVE AVOCADO

i'm an adult . . . kinda.

More like an adult cat.
Like, someone should
probably check in on me,
but i can kinda
make it on my own.

And i'll probably pretend
like i don't need
or want the attention
(even though i do).

There are things you should enjoy now (like staying up late, trying new hobbies, and road trips), and things you should save to enjoy for later (like the newest gadget, high-quality furniture, and all-inclusive vacations).

I PRETEND TO LIKE PEOPLE EVERY DAY. 😎

It's called being an adult, and that is why we are allowed to buy alcohol.

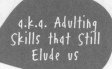
SORTING LAUNDRY

i know this is hard to believe, but clothing manufacturers put care instructions on the tags for a reason. if you don't want to deal with extra hassle, make sure to buy clothes that can be washed similarly.

(Tip: Linen can NOT be washed in hot water or dried unless you want your shirt to fit a doll after doing the laundry.)

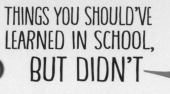

Launderlust

TO YEARN FOR SOMEONE ELSE TO DO YOUR LAUNDRY.

* ALLYSON COOK *

How To Sort Laundry

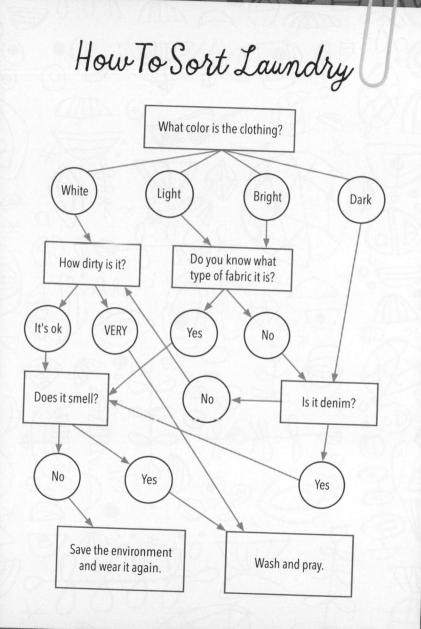

"I'm gonna just make it up as I go."

—ME, about something i should DEFINITELY not make up

#youdoyou

THERE ARE 20-YEAR-OLD
PROFESSIONAL ATHLETES
AND I
STILL PUT MY SHIRT
ON BACKWARDS SOMETIMES.

#ootd
#adulting

THANK YOU INTERNET,
FOR MAKING ME
THE ADULT I AM TODAY.

(Because, in my dad's words,
"There's a YouTube video
for everything these days!")

There are things you should stock your first place with, even if it seems like an expensive hassle, because you never realize you need these things until you REALLY need them:

- scissors and tape (if you're going to get one kind of tape, go for duct tape)
- a can opener
- a corkscrew and bottle opener (surprise: not all bottles are twist-offs)
- a lighter or matches
- bandages
- toilet paper (always a good idea)

#essentials

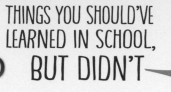
COOKING HACKS

in school, i learned about everything from the mineral hardness scale to theories in 19th century Restoration literature. But i never learned basic cooking skills (which would have benefitted me much more than being able to quote the quadratic equation from memory—but here we are). i still have to call home every time i attempt a new recipe to get tips from Mom.

For those of us who still struggle with the most basic of kitchen skills, here are a few tips to get you going.

DON'T
Put a whole egg in the microwave—a quick way to make a big mess!

DO
Scramble an egg in a bowl before microwaving it—a quick way to make scrambled eggs!

DON'T
Waste any leftover wine (if there IS any left over).

DO
Make wine cubes by pouring any leftover wine into ice cube trays. These can be used to chill future glasses of wine or in a recipe.

DON'T
Let your cutting board slide all over the counter.

DO
Place a wet paper towel or hand towel under your cutting board to give it stability while chopping. (Keep those fingers safe! How else will you post your delicious meal on Instagram?)

PROS AND CONS OF
FREE WILL + FREE TIME

PRO	CON
You can do ANYTHING you want, WHENEVER you want.	it's easy to get distracted and get off track from your goals, over and OVER again.

* Try to cross at least one thing off your "adult-to-dos" before lounging the rest of the day. You'll feel a bit more accomplished

I WANT TIME TO COLOR,
EAT A SNACK,
AND TAKE A NAP.

Basically, i want to be
in kindergarten.

AH YES,
ANOTHER FINE DAY
RUINED BY
RESPONSIBILITY.

You never realize just how quickly a month goes by until you start paying bills.

AGAIN? ALREADY?!

Don't lose your drive.

It's so easy to get caught up in the day-to-day of responsibilities that we can get stuck in a rut—like a video stuck buffering in the middle of playing. Laundry and dishes and errands are never-ending, but try not to get so caught up in the monotony of life that you forget to move forward. Find little moments to invest in your passions, which will refuel your spirit and help get you through the day-to-day with eagerness. Life offers too many incredible opportunities and adventures to live year after year doing the same ol' things.

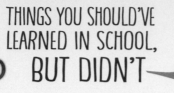

BALANCE YOUR PRIORITIES

Balancing priorities is one of the hardest skills to learn. And it's hard to determine which priorities come first, and which fall lower on the list. This also isn't something that a book can help you with—each person is different in what they value and where they feel they should allocate their time. But here are a few reminders:

TO-DO LIST

Madness Monday
Taco Tuesday
Waffle Wednesday
Thirsty Thursday
Fried Food Friday
Sleep-in Saturday
Sunday Funday

Friendships take effort.
But that effort pays off tremendously.

Don't stress yourself out now over
something that won't matter in a year.

You may not prioritize your specific job,
but your work ethic should matter.

Taco Tuesday is always a priority.

THINGS WE'RE PROBABLY TOO OLD FOR,
BUT HAVEN'T GROWN OUT OF YET:

- Staying up way too late
- Eating too much
- Eating whatever you want
- Saying curse words at inappropriate times
- Not changing your sheets for a long, long time
- Letting the dishes stack up

#sorrynotsorry

Take care of yourself.
Your health and mental
well-being should be
your top priority.

You can find a way to afford what you want, whatever that is—a new tv, plane tickets, a fancy kitchen gadget, etc.

The catch is that you may not be able to afford it RIGHT NOW, but if you set aside just a little bit of money each month, you can stop putting your money towards a bunch of small things and buy that big thing you're dreaming of.

And really, which do you want more? Avocado toast, or the chance to own a house? (Or how about some avocado toast on the beach? Or just avocado toast?)

INCOME

PAYCHECKS/WAGES : $

EXTRA INCOME : $

TOTAL INCOME : $

EXPENSES

RENT : $

UTILITIES : $

TRANSPORTATION : $

GROCERIES : $

LOANS : $

INSURANCE : $

SAVINGS : $

ENTERTAINMENT : $

EATING OUT : $

SPENDING/SHOPPING : $

OTHER : $

TOTAL EXPENSES : $

BALANCE

INCOME – EXPENSES: $

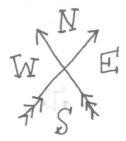

Sometimes, i feel like i should check in with someone and let them know where i'm going... and then i remember that

I'M AN ADULT

and it's pretty awesome.

There are child prodigies
and I still can't
figure out what size
storage container to
put leftovers in.

#winning

WORK VS. PLAY

Sometimes, life is hard and you have to do work.

Work isn't always fun. But part of being an adult means not getting to do the fun stuff all the time, and having to put in the hours. And that's okay. We're full of energy and enthusiasm to prove ourselves most days. But on those days when work seems to be taking up a good chunk of your life, remind yourself of this: you are not your job. And if it's taking up more of your free time than it should, then there's either something wrong with your job or something wrong with how you're doing your job.

I DON'T WANT TO ADULT TODAY.

I don't even want to
human today.

Today, I want to dog.

I'll be laying on the
floor in the sun.
Please pet me and
BRING SNACKS.

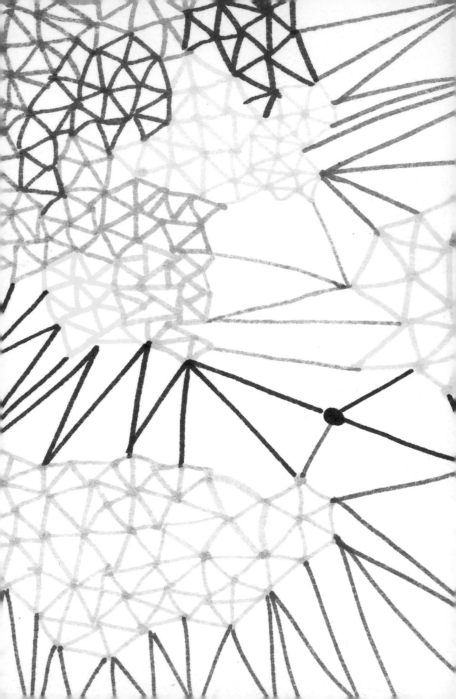

Being an adult is AWESOME, once you've mastered the art of it (or at least given it a good effort). So with these tips and encouragement in mind, go forth and be an adult! And then reward yourself with some fruit gummies.

Or a long, healthy run.

Or both.

WHATEVER, it's YOUR adulthood.
Do whatever you want!

If you enjoyed this book
or it has touched your life
in some way, we'd love to
hear from you.

Please write a review at
Hallmark.com, e-mail us at
booknotes@hallmark.com,
or send your comments to:

Hallmark Book Feedback
P.O. Box 419034
Mail Drop 100
Kansas City, MO 64141